A TALE FROM THE LAND OF STORIES

THE CURVY TREE

BY CHRIS COLFER

ILLUSTRATED BY BRANDON DORMAN

LB

LITTLE, BROWN AND COMPANY

NEW YORK BOSTON

Once upon a time, a little girl ran away from her village in tears.

With nowhere to go, and no one to talk to, she ran into the forest to be alone. She ran and ran until her feet grew tired, so she looked for a place to sit.

Most of the woods had been cleared out by loggers, but in the very center of all the stumps was a curvy tree standing alone. He was different from all the other trees she had ever seen. His roots were winding, his trunk was curled, and his branches looped toward the sky.

The little girl was so sad, she didn't even notice the strange tree. She sat under its shade and cried so much that a puddle of tears formed on the ground below her.

The Curvy Tree was awoken from his afternoon nap by her cries. He was troubled to see such a small girl acting so sad, so he bent down to make sure she was all right.

"Little girl, why are you crying?" the Curvy Tree asked.

"You can talk?" the little girl said with a fright.

The Curvy Tree nodded. "I can."

"Do all trees talk?" she asked.

"When they have something to say, I suppose," the Curvy Tree said. "We can talk, laugh, sing—and cry when we're feeling blue. That's why I'm wondering what's troubling you."

"The other children in my village are very mean to me," the little girl said with a sniffle. "They make fun of my glasses and they tease me about my hair. They say that I talk funny, I'm not pretty, and I'm not smart."

"That's silly," the tree said. "I'm just a tree and even I can see that isn't true. Those village children would be lucky to have a friend like you."

"No matter how nice I am, they're never nice to me," the little girl said. "I don't think I'm ever going to find a friend."

The Curvy Tree wiped her tears with his leaves. He thought about her troubles and was reminded of something that had happened a very long time ago.

"May I tell you a story? I think it will make you feel better."

"What story could make me feel better?" the little girl asked.

"It's my story," the tree said. "When I was young, barely taller than a shrub, the other trees in the woods were very mean to me because I was different."

"They made fun of my winding roots, my curvy trunk, and my loopy branches. It made me sad, and I used to cry myself to sleep every night."

"Then one day, loggers came to the forest and cut down all the trees except for me."

"They thought I was too curvy to be a chair, too twisty for a table, and too loopy for a house, so they left me all alone in the woods. Being different may have been difficult, but it's what saved me."

"But didn't you get lonely without the other trees?" the little girl asked.

"Indeed I did," the tree said. "I thought I would be alone forever. But then I grew, and I grew, and then I grew some more. I grew so tall that I could see far into the distance, and it made me smile."

"Why?" the little girl asked. "What did you see?"

The Curvy Tree scooped up the little girl. He raised her high into the sky so she could see for herself. In the distance, all around them, were dozens of curvy trees in other forests. They all waved and smiled at the little girl. And standing on their branches were other children.

"Those children are all just like me!"
the little girl said with a smile.

"You may feel different and you may feel alone, but one day you'll grow and discover that there are many friends to be found if you look past the horizon," the tree said.

"There's no reason to cry, for, you see, in every forest there's a curvy tree."

ABOUT THIS BOOK

This book was edited by Alvina Ling and Bethany Strout
and designed by Kristina Iulo. The production was supervised by
Erika Schwartz, and the production editor was Andy Ball. The illustrations for
this book were composed digitally, and the book was printed on 128 gsm Gold Sun
matte paper. The text and the display type were set in Bulmer MT.

Little, Brown and Company

Hachette Book Group
1290 Avenue of the Americas, New York, NY 10104
Visit us at lb-kids.com

Little, Brown and Company is a division of Hachette Book Group, Inc.
The Little, Brown name and logo are trademarks of Hachette Book Group, Inc.

The publisher is not responsible for websites (or their content) that are not owned by the publisher.

First Edition: October 2015

Library of Congress Cataloging-in-Publication Data
Colfer, Chris, 1990–
The Curvy Tree / by Chris Colfer ; illustrated by Brandon Dorman.—First edition.
pages cm
Summary: A friendless girl who is teased for being different runs away from her village in tears and finds herself having a conversation with a
very unusual tree, who tells a story of how his differences not only saved his life,
they helped him see that he is not so very different after all.
ISBN 978-0-316-40685-7 (hardcover)—ISBN 978-0-316-29942-8 (ebook) [1. Individuality—Fiction.
2. Self-acceptance—Fiction.
3. Trees—Fiction. 4. Youths' writings.] I. Dorman, Brandon, illustrator. II. Title.
PZ7.C677474Cur 2015
[E]—dc23
2014041121

10 9 8 7 6 5 4 3 2 1
APS
PRINTED IN CHINA